A Brain that Couldn't Be Broken

by

His Grace Through Traumatic Brain Trauma

The contents of this work, including, but not limited to, the accuracy of events, people, and places depicted; opinions expressed; permission to use previously published materials included; and any advice given or actions advocated are solely the responsibility of the author, who assumes all liability for said work and indemnifies the publisher against any claims stemming from publication of the work.

All Rights Reserved
Copyright © 2018 by His Grace Through Traumatic Brain Trauma

No part of this book may be reproduced or transmitted, downloaded, distributed, reverse engineered, or stored in or introduced into any information storage and retrieval system, in any form or by any means, including photocopying and recording, whether electronic or mechanical, now known or hereinafter invented without permission in writing from the publisher.

Dorrance Publishing Co
585 Alpha Drive
Suite 103
Pittsburgh, PA 15238
Visit our website at *www.dorrancebookstore.com*

ISBN: 978-1-4809-2538-0
eISBN: 978-1-4809-2307-2

December 9th 1987

A brain that couldn't be broken.

On a Thursday morning, I woke up at Cooper's Hospital for trauma in Camden, New Jersey from being in a coma, not knowing that I had been involved in a serious car accident. The only thought inside my mind was, "How did I get in a hospital bed?" when I usually wake up in my bed at my home. I decided to use the telephone to call my wife and find out from her why I was in the hospital and how did I get there.

When I spoke with her, she stated to me, "You were involved in a serious car accident. It caused you to be unconscious."

My reply back was: "Come get me; I'm alright. My place is to be at home, not here in a hospital room."

"I'll come and visit you tomorrow."

Once I hung up the phone, a nurse walked into the room to give me medication. All I could ask of this nurse was, "What is the purpose for taking this medicine?"

Her response was it helped keep me calm. The only thing I wanted to keep me calm was my wife, using her sweet love and affection. The nurse then put two pills in my hand and a cup of water. Around forty-five minutes later, I began to notice my thoughts ripidly changed and I just couldn't seem to get myself to slow down for some apparent reason. I sat next to the window, looking at the traffic going across the Benjamin Franklin Bridge and into the City of Brotherly Love, which is Philadelphia, Pennsylvania, where I was born and raised. Everything seemed so different from the way it used to be in my life.

What was wrong with me so much that I had to be in a hospital? I could only notice my right ankle was puffed out, and when I looked in a mirror, my left eye had a lump above my eyelashes.

I was still wondering to myself how this all happened so suddenly to me a few days later. I had several questions I had to ask the doctor in charge of this ward, but all I continued to hear was that I had been in a bad accident and needed to start taking physical therapy for my left arm and right ankle. After several days, I met with other patients around the hospital. Some of them let me know they were involved in accidents also.

Around bedtime, the nurse approached me again to take more medicine. I refused, and she walked out. Fifteen minutes later, there were two security officers at my bedside asking me why I refused to take the medication. Next, they said that they would have to strap me to the bed.

My response: "If you do such a thing, I'm going to contact the state attorney general's office, and when I finish getting all the answers to this bullshit, my personal lawyer will take care of the rest of the complaint I have with this place. No one is giving me any reason why I need to be in a hospital taking medication."

After having no communication at this hospital, my insurance company decided to send me to Moss Rehabilitation in Philadelphia. I felt good knowing that I would be going to the state I was raised in. Nevertheless, no one could explain to me what my problem was, so I kept on believing nothing was wrong.

I was admitted on a Sunday. Everyone was very pleasant at Moss. The nurses and I began to get along. It took a little time to get along with a few of the patients; also the doctor at this rehabilitation center was difficult. I felt now was the time to start asking lots of questions. One special part of my brain that didn't get damaged was my communication skills. I never had any trouble talking with people, and I've always loved to talk and make friends with people since the six grade. A few of my teachers from my school days said they enjoyed having me in their classes. Mrs. Jones, Mrs. Morales, Mrs. Mitchell, all from my middle school days, helped me be successful with picking and choosing my class friends; they also made sure I got all of my assignments completed before moving on. Mr. Larkin and Mr. Fret were my high school buddies and that for sure kept me on track with all my high school activities to get better with any leadership programs for graduation.

As I began to get familiar with Moss Rehab, I just kept thinking nothing was wrong with me. So I phoned my wife and told her I wanted to come home, and she replied that we should speak with the head doctor in charge, which was Dr. Mayer. I had a gut feeling that he would say no, I couldn't go home at this time, and that's what he stated to her. I was thankful to know that I could only go home overnight, but had to return the next day. I then developed a bad attitude, started cursing at the doctor and nurses. I am so sure my wife did hear what was going on in, the background while on the phone!

"No, Sam you can't go home permanently at this time." However he stated to her "He's able to go home for an overnight visit but he has to return."

Several hours later, she came to get me. Again, the main idea I had was to go home and start finding out what the problem was with me since no one could give me any information concerning my injuries. When I did find the free time, I made phone calls to gather what information I could. A few days later, I went to my mother's residence, not believing that it was going to be uncomfortable, but something was totally wrong. All of a sudden, I just could not stand any noise from kids. I knew that something was the matter with me because I've always been able to put up with loud noise and sounds from kids or just about anything. Suddenly, my son was very in shock to see his father this way; he became afraid to talk with me.

He continued to repeat, "Dad, the reason you act this way is because you were hurt in a car accident, and it hurt your head."

Two days later the township police came to my mother's home telling us a neighbor complained someone threw trash on their lawn, saying it was me, who passed by their property and saw me littering. The police man wanted to enter the house, I refused and stepped out the door to talk with Officer Grimes. I did notice his police badge. As I reached the bottom of the steps, he grabbed me and tried to put hand cuffs on me.

The next words from my mouth were, "You will be sorry for this shit."

At this time, Officer Grimes said, "I have to take you in. I was informed you have been in an auto accident. All I need is a few questions from you, then you can go back home."

My concern at the time was to telephone my attorney so I could find out why the law could hold someone responsible for something that they truly didn't cause themselves. Once I reached my attorney, he let me know not to worry about anything. He said he would have me out of police custody right away. Shortly after getting back to my mother's home, I called my wife to come pick me up. She relied that she could not right at the moment, she said "I prefer you get escorted back home by authorities."

I said "How about my great true friend Evans who can drive me there?"

"No," she said, "I'd rather an officer bring you to our house."

I said, "Honey, what's wrong with your thinking? Do you think your husband is a criminal or rapist, just because the cops arrested me?"

Her next reply: "Your accident really did hurt you, and you don't realize it. You need someone to help you understand what's going on inside of your brain."

About all I could say was, "This is a bunch of nonsense, bullshit. I can handle myself. I'm not a child."

Her only answer was, "I'm looking around for a good rehab so you can get back to your normal way of reasoning."

The only person who would let me know what happened was my mother Margaret Sherman. She informed me who, what, when, where, this injury took place, and she stated, "You were hit by a man driving a pickup truck. He was taking supplies to New York that evening. You were unconscious. I prayed for you all night when I heard that you were in a car accident."

My mother explained to me that she had a talk with God about this problem and asked him to wake me up out of this coma. Also, I was told our family came together and prayed for me. The next day, I went home to be with my wife. Things were going smooth until I arrived at the house. She wouldn't answer the door, so I went to look for a telephone. When I called her, we begin to argue. The only words from her mouth that she could tell her husband was I want a police officer to escort you here, so I went to the township police department of Willingboro, New Jersey, to get an officer to escort me to my residence. Minutes after arriving to my residence, the officer, my wife and myself sat down and discussed the main issue of why she felt I would always need law enforcement to escort me to my own property.

"What have I done to deserve this trouble?" Next statement from her was that I would not be staying home because something was wrong with my brain. The question I was curious about was how did anyone know what was going on inside of my brain. "Not any of you are brain specialists."

"Samuel, you had a bad accident which caused you a traumatic brain injury."

Next, I mentioned to this officer, "Why am I not damaged all over my body? I feel just fine. Once in a while I feel strange, but for some odd reason I just feel a little tired most of the time now."

Once I would get rest, it seemed as though my mind went through so many anger stages. My wife and stepkids seemed to look at me in the strangest ways. They said, "Dad you're crazy; that accident really hurt your head." I said to them "prove to me I had been in a car accident, maybe then I could believe what everyone was saying."

Days later, I received a phone call from an attorney that I never spoke with. He told me that he would be handling my case for this accident. He then expressed to me, "Samuel, your wife had me visit you at the hospital and you did a form to let me represent you and your family."

I made a great effort towards this attorney to say "I never signed anything for you to be my lawyer," but he then brought up that my wife was right there and witnessed me signing the form so he could handle my injury case. I continued to refuse this statement, then I let him know next I would be contacting my original attorney in Woodbury, New Jersey, to find out about this so-called form that I supposedly had signed.

"I don't remember signing any form. If I did this, I must have been totally unconscious."

I went upstairs to watch my afternoon game shows, *Password, Card Sharks*, and *$25,000 Pyramid*. Soon she came up the steps to tell me she had errands to run, and asked if would I like anything from the store. I told her I wanted something from Arby's, also to stop by the men's hair supply store and pickup some S-Curl hair spray.

She said, "It will be late when I get back."

"Well, I'll just walk there and buy it myself."

"You cannot go anywhere alone; your head isn't in the best condition right now. For the time being, it is better for you to be close to home. Whatever the insurance company say's at this point, that's where you'll go," Kathy said to me. "I am in contact with a good rehab nurse from your car insurance company to find a place for your kind of trauma.

"Hun, you cannot stay at this house with this kind of condition; can you not tell you need help? The way things are with your attitude and behavior, it's not good at all. You're not acting like my husband anymore, even the kids notice you have changed."

Next I picked up the telephone and called my best friend Evans to get further understanding about this injury.

"Why does everyone feel as though I'm a bad person all of a sudden?"

He went over the accident with me.

"A pickup truck hit your Honda Accord head on and knocked you unconscious. So what happened is your head was banged around very bad."

"Well, how come I still feel good, just as I've always felt?"

"You're still a great person, Samuel, but at this present time, you do not quite realize how much your head got hurt. It's good you're still alive and talking. At times you act strange, more than before your brain injury. We all notice that you get out of control. All you need is for someone professional to help you get back to feeling normal."

My true best friend, Evans always gave me good advice. He has known about my ups and downs for eighteen years. We both treat one another with a lot of respect. The one thing he continued to say was, "You need to get yourself together before you can do anything."

After our nice conversation, I phoned my Aunt Amy in Philadelphia to see if she knew anything on this so-called traumatic accident. Suddenly, Kathy came into the kitchen and asked who was I talking with.

"Don't you be calling long-distance on my phone. Absolutely no one came to see you in the hospital."

I said to my wife, "Maybe they never knew anything about an accident I had."

She mentioned, "There will be a live in sitter with you soon, Hun, to watch what you do every day."

I told Kathy, "Sweetheart, you must be a little off in your own mind too, to think someone needs to be looking over me. I can take care of myself; I've been doing that since I moved out on my own. So don't think someone is going to be living here, in my house, getting involved with my personal business. If I need any help, I'll go see someone on my own. The only help I prefer is from God above. He has more power to pull me through than any man on this Earth.

"Whatever's wrong with me, God will fix it and make it better. All we need is faith."

The next sentence my wife Kathy spoke was, "I'll still be getting help from somewhere for you Hun. If you only knew how much you have changed since your accident."

Two weeks later, I had a bad dispute with my wife and mother on not being able to make decisions for myself. I did use the phone at my mother's home, calling Kathy saying a few curse words to her.

"I will come for you and bring you home," Kathy said. "I hope, things will work this time, you have lots of anger that you didn't have before. That is the reason I want to get help for you. The trauma unit did a great job with your left eye. They took you to the best in the Delaware Valley.

All I could say was, "Honey, it doesn't feel like anything is wrong. I just need love. Something is wrong with our marriage; you have been changing for the past month now, and I cannot figure out why you just won't talk to me. It's starting to feel like, we're not even a married couple. What we need from this marriage is the two of us try to understand what we're both going through."

A few days later, I received a call from Sue Emerick. She explained her job as a rehab nurse from Hanover Insurance Company.

"I'm calling to give you a better understanding of what happened to you. Ever since this injury occurred, your reaction and thinking isn't the same around people. Mr. Sherman, you have sustained a brain trauma, which caused your memory to become bad. Also, your impulse control isn't stable right now. So we're going to get you into a great treatment program.

"I was called by your wife. She wants me to find help for you, Mr. Sherman, right away."

My only words were, "Prove to me I had an accident. Send some proven facts on how this all happened before I get sent anywhere. First, I would like for you to start talking with my attorney, then he can inform me on the best decision to make. Please don't bother me until you discuss all this information with my attorney."

I personally phoned my lawyer to let him know I had just spoke with Hanover Insurance Company.

"A treatment nurse named Sue Emerick called me to say, they're working on a rehabilitation program for my kind of injury. I've never seen any kind of evidence or proof to let me know about any traumatic trauma that I've been involved in, nor anything that stated I was hurt from an accident. Could you please gather more information from the insurance to be sure whichever treatment facility they come across can be in the state of Pennsylvania or New Jersey? I prefer not to be traveling too far from my home."

I was aware enough to recall, did my present law firm know any details on the Rosenberg firm who con me into signing papers for that firm to handle my case? I wanted my case out of their hands, so I brought to my lawyer's attention take whatever action needed to get my case and files to their office. I don't want any other firm to represent me at all.

"Do all you can to help me. Send a letter right away to that firm."

Mr. Angelini said to me, "You need not worry. From this point on, I'll make sure your file gets to my office. If Mr. Rosenberg refuses to release your file, I can take further legal action to get the file, Sam. Nevertheless, I will, continue finding out all the details of your accident for you. Your file is just as good as already on my desk!"

Built up inside of me was a lot of anger in which I had never experienced before. It felt as though most of the people around me made things so uncomfortable. All I could say to anyone was, "Just leave me alone."

The only person I could stand talking with was my grandfather. He always shared a lot of love. Both my mother and my wife would make me feel so dissatisfied when they approached me for any kind of communication. Kathy just kept saying that I didn't know what I was talking about. Mom said I needed to be by myself, to stay away from everyone right now and not talk with many people.

"Just trust in God. He is going to bring you through all the frustration inside of your brain, along with some professional help. As my son, I want you to get help. You're not the same, Son, since your head was hit. Something inside of your mind is telling you that you're okay, but your head was hit pretty hard. As time goes by you'll understand what I really mean." As my Grandson, I want you to get help. You're not the same anymore since your head was hit.

My family and friends kept calling my mother's home to tell me I'm blessed to be alive. All I could say was, "how come I don't notice anything wrong with me?" I only noticed my left arm in a cast and my right ankle was puffed out. Now I was saying to myself, "Do these two things make me not know how to handle my own responsibilities? Why does everyone think against me this way now? I'm not a kid. What's the problem? I don't need anyone's sympathy. All I want is cooperation." The only person who seemed to give me their love and cooperation was my grandfather. Joe Morgan was his name. He knew the right things to say to help me feel positive, and without his love and concern, several times I would have said curse words to family and friends. My main problem was I needed someone to let me know what's going on, but it seemed as though the more I tried to find out, everyone turned me away. This made me feel like people thought I was crazy.

Minute by minute, everyone seemed to be isolating themselves away from me. Each new day I felt like I needed to take a vacation, somewhere like the South Pacific, Canada, or the Philippines. There were certain factors I had to consider, having a wife with stepchildren sort of made it unrealistic to try to take a vacation at the moment. My true blood son continued saying, "Dad you need to get help from somewhere. You're for certain not like you used to be since your head got hurt. All of us in the family are afraid now when you do raise your voice. This never happened before, that's the reason I know you're not the same person you were before this traumatic experience.

"Dad, you have changed quite a bit. I'm personally praying for someone to help you get back to your normal living ways. Neighbors are scared of you, and my friends keep saying, 'what is wrong with your dad? He acting so strange now."

My son said he felt so bad to hear this from friends and certain neighbors, it made him a little angry. Going through a trauma inside your brain isn't easy to understand. Most of the time, you don't even realize or remember what you're doing with yourself or towards others. This is why I was treated so negative. I am a grown man, and I didn't like being misled as if I was a child. Whatever the problem in my life, God will make a way out of no way. I've always heard that faith can move mountains.

For some apparent reason, my thoughts were mixed up. On sunny nice days, my grandfather and I would sit outside in the backyard under the beautiful pine tree and discuss this problem. It was so odd; I just couldn't notice anything wrong inside of my mind. There were days I felt just as normal as I had always been and others where I felt angry and confused. At certain times of the day, it would take at least fifteen minutes to settle down from all the agitation inside of me, but I never could relate to why would I get so angry.

A great neighbor of ours, my mother's best girlfriend, Esther, would stop by and see me after she would get off from work at the middle school she taught at in the township were we resided. The first comment from her: "You're going to beat all of this. It's going to take some faith and time, but you'll be on your merry way again."

I said to her, "Mrs. Pierison, you have always been a very positive person, ever since I've known you. I'm glad to hear you say all of these good things. It does let me know somebody really cares since this has happened."

The only positive information I could ever feel relaxed with was from my grandfather, along with Mrs. Pierision, at any time day or night.

One afternoon a counselor came to my mother's home to ask about any special interests I had. He brought up areas in my life that could be worked on. After a head trauma, everything changes. You might not think so, but my life is much different now. I mentioned to this gentleman that noticed, at times, that I repeated myself more than I did before. But somehow, I felt like I could do a lot of things all at once.

Gerald stated, "This program will get you started to recovery." When I asked how much would it cost, he answered, "approximately $3,300."

It was good I had insurance; they had lots of money to put out for many different things. But it didn't matter to me if they were willing to pay this amount of funds. No one could give me any clues on how this started; about all I could get out of anyone was "we want to help you feel better." Anger started to enter my mind. Why did people want to help me so much? It felt as if I won the million-dollar lottery, or did I receive an outstanding salesman awards from the state of New Jersey? Laughter is what I had. Was everyone trying to play a joke on me? Why wasn't anyone giving me a straight answer?

Within the next day or two, I received a phone call from my attorney. He let me know the best way I could get the results of what took place and why I was in this condition. I was still handling myself professionally to get all the results accomplished.

A few of my co-workers told me, "Samuel, it's hard to believe you have been in a trauma unit. You seem as normal as anyone else."

I got back in touch with my attorney.

Mr. Angelini said, "Sam, I'm glad to represent you with this case. I've always wanted you to become a part of this law firm. You have been a people-person ever since I've known you. I have had some conversations with some of the corporations you have worked for, and all of their replies were positive on how much of an effective communicator you are with others.

"But now, at the moment, your communication skills have been affected since your accident. There are several other areas of your brain that have some damage, but I won't know this information until you attend a very thorough treatment facility. Sam, you're still a bright young man, and I'm thinking you shouldn't be a part of any treatment facility too long, just enough time to locate the main difficulties going on inside of your brain. What we are after, Sam, is getting you quality help so you can get back to all of the normal functions of your life."

My attorney continued to say, "Sam, I know it makes you angry having so many people making decisions for you right now. I will get working on your case right away; it won't take very long because you have a great insurance company this time to settle with, so you can cheer up about that at least. We can settle things up in one to two years. They have smart claims representatives to work along with. No doubt, Sam, you're covered well with benefits from Hanover Insurance. They're the best around.

"First we need to contact the bank in Florida who owns your car. When that's out of the way, it's going to be a pleasure to work on your file. Just go along with your rehab nurse, do whatever Hanover wants, and you best believe this will turn out in your favor. This law firm will fight for you anyway we can. As I told you before my reputation with most of the county judges has been outstanding. So you don't have to be afraid of anything. Once you take some very good rehabilitation, everyone will hopefully stop saying you don't know what you're talking about. The people that know you realize your life expectations are fine, but the kind of accident that occurred would cause anyone a lot of confusion, Sam."

Later on, I returned to my mother's home, checked the mail box and I noticed there was a letter from the Willingboro Township Police Department. The letter mentioned Burlington County officers would be coming to Lawnside to arrest me for cursing and slapping my wife. My reaction was that I wanted to leave and take a vacation in the Pocano Moutains in up-state Pennsylvania. Don't run off trying to take a vacation, face the troubles in front of you at the present time, and stop looking at things in the past. What's done is done. Never look back, face the future. You'll never understand what is wrong until you get the correct help and medicine to get your circumstances under control.

"Believe it or not, your brain is still functional. You know how to help and speak with other human beings. Good, true facts are what you need about your brain injury, Sam."

A week or two later, my wonderful grandfather continued to talk to me, saying, "You don't act the same. That's the reason I tell you you're not the same, grandson. Something is wrong inside your mind. But I'm glad you have a very decent lawyer. He's one of the best in the Delaware Valley and the state of New Jersey. I'm quite sure you'll get the best results with a man who has God in his heart.

"What's more important, grandson, is listening to what people have to say or doing what God wants you to do. Grandson, don't waste time fooling around in the devil's mess; just pray and trust in God, as I keep telling you. No man can get by what God has planned. You will get through this accident. God is on the throne. He'll see you through. Try to go along with how they want to help you get better. Don't let anything trouble your mind. Whatever the problem is, Jesus will fix it. Just trust Him.

"All I will continue to tell you, grandson, is keep trusting in the word of God, and everything else will come to pass."

Right after my conversation with my grandfather, I received a telephone call from my wife. She stated to me she been told not to let me stay at home with her and the kids.

"I miss you, darling, and Talia always likes when I read her bedtime stories," I said. "Your husband misses our good conversations, also your loving care. I'm sure you miss all of our loving care together as husband and wife. All of my family is asking about you."

At the time, I wanted to say to others, "Stop saying I cannot handle making decisions. The accident didn't destroy all of my brain-cells." The only thing I noticed was that I didn't like loud noises or for anyone to keep discussing the same issues. Somehow, I would get so angry that my voice would get louder and then people around me became afraid. All I wanted was for everybody to leave me alone.

It felt like nothing made sense anymore. The only thing I could do was hold my peace as much as I could. There was a lot of anger in my mind, and I had never had this kind of feeling before. Once, my wife had told me she wanted me to leave the house, that I needed help for my brain injury. Her reaction wasn't good; she ran down the, stairs grabbed her coat and purse, went out, got in her car and drove off. No one seemed to care about what I was going through. My wife had changed since this accident has taken place. When Kathy returned, my reaction still wasn't at its best. She informed me that she went to speak with some people who will be able to help me out.

Suddenly, it felt very good to talk with the kids after watching television. I went upstairs to read a bedtime story to Talia, and everything was going just right like it always used to. My wife Kathy was making me feel at home again. She ironed my clothes and fixed me breakfast in bed. We went over all of our financial matters, and this was sort of getting some of the tension in my mind under control.

It felt as though since we moved to the township of Willingboro, New Jersey, every minute that went by, my head felt like it had been crushed. It was so difficult to accept the way I felt. The kids kept telling me to stay upstairs because of my right leg. The only time I should go downstairs was to eat or when we went out. She made me feel helpless. I would walk downstairs to see the kids off to school. At times, I would go outdoors to look around the house. The main idea was to exercise my mind from all insanity.

No one wanted to listen, but I had ideas of my own to help myself feel better. I felt under pressure in all directions. I kept myself feeling good regardless of what everyone would say by talking to those who knew my pattern of living. When I got the chance, I went to talk with important, high people. The professionals that I touched base with all said, "I couldn't imagine this kind of injury happening to you, Samuel. You look the same to all of us. Can you remember who hit your car?"

I explained to my ex-co-workers and my friends, "It doesn't seem as though anything happened to me. I only noticed that my right ankle was bruised and my left arm was in a cast, but nothing else seems wrong."

Folks kept telling me my head was hit hard.

"Somehow your thinking isn't the same. You should talk with a brain trauma doctor," they said. No one knew how it felt to continuously hear the same old words day in and day out. It made me upset every time someone said that my thinking wasn't good. My answer to those who felt this way about me was to say, "It's a disgrace to the Creator to say bad things towards others, especially when you really don't know the true story about a person life."

There's a family two doors down from my mother's house, which I would go to daily, mainly because the spirit of the Lord was always present in that house. Mrs. Sunkett made me feel welcome at any time. Whenever you walk inside of their door, if you're a saved person, the sprit of God would come upon your soul. Religious gospel music. Several great ministers, such as Charles Stanley, Pastor Jerry Farwell, and Reverand Shambach, would help my troubles inside of my weary mind and soul vanished, as I would listen to the radio. Just to know the Lord in your own life makes things much easier to handle.

Being in this type of condition is a big pain in the rear. No one believed in me anymore. I just wanted to get away and get around new folks who didn't know me. The folks around the township felt there wasn't any hope for me. Suddenly, there were questions asked to my family. Did I have a good insurance company? Did I realize I would need a good lawyer who can take care all of my financial matters? It was about all I could to tell those nosy folks to mind their own damn business. If they didn't, I would curse them out.

This type of outburst I kept going through with many folks began to put me in an uncomfortable attitude. I tried all possibilities that I could to not let this mess bother me. Any kind of noise around me would cause my voice level to increase. I still wonder to myself what made me do such things. It never seemed as though an accident could make things change as it did. Now I began to see for myself that something was wrong. My wife Kathy changed her outlook towards our marriage. She spread rumors to her family members concerning her husband's brain injury. What a fucked up mess. I sat myself down and turned on the radio. The only station I could listen to was relaxing smooth jazz music. It was so interesting hearing instrumental sounds in the background of each song played by different jazz artists.

I purposely took my mind away from any kind of accident. I made myself think about my former job as being a salesman and how much I cared about reaching out to companies to save their operations from using toxic chemicals. My desire was too understand what the problem was with my head. The moment I would hear any uncalled-for subjects about my situation would certainly piss me off. Every day, I felt very uncomfortable when I couldn't remember some thing that was important, but still, I never felt like I had a brain injury. Most of the day, I found myself sitting around for hours thinking of what I needed to remember. For some odd reason, during any part of any day, I would lose control of my thought process and go from one thing to the next, it wouldn't bother or matter to me. But to others, it seemed different to see me handle myself that way, yet with good standards.

Just as I begin to think everything was going smooth to avoid conflicts, I had a bad conversation with my uncle. He said, "Calm yourself down as much as you can." If not, he would come down there and get me and bring me to his job. He stated, "you do know where I work. Trenton State Prison. My nephew, you have to realize your head has been hit. This is what is causing you to do things so much differently now than before. Our family and your friends are very afraid of you and your actions."

I for certain didn't believe what I kept hearing, actually hearing my uncle say this about what the family said. This even had me somewhat scared he was serious. Several days later, he did leave a message to my mother and wife, saying that if I started cursing or doing anything dangerous, he would be down and handcuff me. A couple of weeks later, I was informed that my Uncle Joe will be coming down for the weekend.

Once he arrived, we walked around the block, and he remained to say to his nephew, "Your brain is damaged; you just can't understand what's going on with yourself throughout the day." He told me when I noticed anything starting to get too loud, just get out and take a nice long walk. "That will help all the pressure inside of your brain. Once you get back to the house, find some work to do outside. Any yard work or something to keep your mind busy. Please do not go in the house and sit around. Things will begin to feel as if they're closing in at you. Get yourself out and walk. Those brain tissues have been disturbed. Your mind needs to be free so you can stay calm and relaxed.

"One of the reason's you get so angry is because you're not at work like you used to be. Never for a moment did you like depending on anyone. At the present time you don't have your license to drive. The main source is that you cannot get any money to support yourself. So there is the answer to all of your anger. Go somewhere quiet; it can help you and your thoughts, so they aren't all over the place."

Most of the time, it seemed as though my brain just couldn't slow itself down. I would start doing one thing and just didn't finish it. My mind would be on something else. This would happen all day. The moment I wrote business letters, my brain somehow settled down suddenly. I could come up with ideas for the marketing department at United Laboratories, and also give purchasing agents ways to market their services. About the only time my brain would settle itself was when I found the chance to write notes, letters, business information or school work for the kids, otherwise I would become agitated with everything around me.

My patience wasn't there anymore. I went through so much trouble calming myself down, that's what I disliked the most concerning this injury to my brain. Every day, my mother would call my father's brother who lived down the street from us to talk with me, so I could stay calm, but he also started setting limits. I couldn't quite relate to what my Uncle Budd was doing; never before had he ever approached me like this. Since my father wasn't around anymore, this helped my mother feel a lot more at ease.

One afternoon, my best friend Evans, who I still had much contact with, picked me up. We went to his job to get his paycheck and afterwards went to a carwash. We began to discuss my problems.

"Why does your wife act the way she does towards you? What is the reason your insurance company cannot pay for special treatment or one on one help?" Evans asked. "Let's both look around for a place where you can get someone to examine your head. I'm going to help you as much as I can. Pick a town you want us to begin researching, so you can get better again. Which of the problems should we work on first? Your left arm or right-ankle? Attitude and anger level? Your left eye and blurred vision? tTake your pick of which part of your body you want to work on first."

Evans's suggestion was to get my eye examined. "The other parts of your injuries, you can solve them later by yourself," he said. "Sam, I want your honest opinion. What is your wife Kathy doing about your troubles? Is she sticking right there with you, or does she want you put away somewhere. Sam, you just got married three months ago. I hope things continue to stay smooth and not get rough. A serious problem has happened with your brain that won't be going away like any magic trick.

"Important information was found out through the hospital unit. I need to be aware of anything that can make you upset. I'll be in touch with you, every day. Don't be afraid to look for some help on your own. I know you're not feeling like your old self, but you have to start somewhere."

Weeks later, I heard news that the insurance company found a rehab in Malvern, Pennsylvania. My attorney's office informed me that my insurance company wanted to back out because of the cost. But he said he would keep communicating and staying in touch with all important people at Hanover, until something comes through. Meanwhile, my patience was getting low and worn out. There was no one in sight who could relate to what I wanted and needed. From this point forth, I decided to call the New Jersey State Attorney General in Trenton. Once I received mail from the Attorney General's Office to start a complaint, I discovered it was going to cost $500. My family gave me their support to raise the cash. Many of my family and friends were so surprised by how I could still use my brain to carry on business functions without any assistance. The majority of the time, I noticed my brain moving faster than it usually did, and I just couldn't figure out why everything never slowed itself down. Whatever thought came in my mind, I would do just that one particular thing. It was such a different experience, having head trauma. I noticed how my attitude was very poor towards any conditions and had never had this problem before. All along, I was trying to make myself believe I had a head trauma, which was just even more disrupting.

Daily, I would think of my former work. As a salesman, I began feeling just like my own normal self. My former boss at United Labs, Jay Cohen, saw me and said, "Sam, the way you look and sound, you could go right to work at your desk again. We sure do miss that great sales ability of yours for our corporation." Jay ask me if I knew what my main problem was that kept me from working.

"It would be nice if you could show a few of the new salesman what the first approach should be when selling to customers," he said. "Your style of industrial sales has never been used this way."

Supervisor George Nitche stated, "When you recover from your injury, we want you to return to work at United Labortories. Our accounting office in Addision, Illinois told us they noticed no sales coming in from P-17-M desk Samuel Sherman."

One of the secretaries mentioned what she enjoyed about me as a salesman for the corporation. I used a unique way to get in reach with several companies from the past that none of the other salesman could ever succeed at doing. At an executive level meeting with a few area managers, they saw I still had sales skills and experience.

Each time I spoke about doing my job again, my wife Kathy said it would be difficult now because I talked too fast and no one would listen to me. Whenever I crossed my wife, she would get on the phone with my insurance company and tell them I needed an evaluation A.S.A.P. Nothing like this had ever happened under these circumstances. None of this made any sense what-so-ever;

nothing seemed to work as it used to in my life. That afternoon, I was alone at the house trying hard not to continue making myself feel upset. Any time someone told me I was wrong about anything, it would trigger my frontal lobe and make me so agitated and confused. At any particular point of the conversation, I would find myself using bad words to get my point across to anyone.

When night came around, I would never get much sleep; I kept dreaming about hurting any person who ever treated me wrong. I just couldn't get any kind of agreements between my stepchildren and I. As for myself, I felt like junk, useless, and my thoughts felt horrible. All together this nightmare was bad as hell. Once every now and then, I would hear friends and family say that I still do several things the same way I did before this injury happened, but nevertheless all I saw was un-for-sure individuals making uncertain criticisms, not realizing all of the chaos going on inside my brain. About the only thing that would help clear my mind and the negative feelings was to watch MTV or look at my favorite game shows, *$100,000 Pyramid*, *Password*, *Card Sharks*, and *Love Connection*.

Lord knows my brain just didn't feel comfortable every single time I looked at my left eye in the mirror. It was so different from the rest of my face, and this made me think that something was wrong with my brain. Not even knowing all my legal rights, I had changed. Not a single soul could give me the information I figured it out for myself. Slowly, I began understanding a little better when I questioned my attorney on certain subjects. A couple of the medications were starting to bring my thoughts in order. Believe me, it was not easy to share any of my main concerns about my personal affairs with professional people anymore.

Most of the time I felt guilty every day, but this accident wasn't my fault. I had to suffer the consequences because of someone else's mistake. All I was told was a man driving a pick-up truck taking merchandise to New York caused the accident on December 9, 1987. I saw a news clipping showing the accident. The man who hit my car was named was James Manny; he was highly intoxicated, and the pickup he drove hit the median in the center part of the highway then flipped over onto my Honda Accord. Now after seeing and hearing this shocking news report, I was informed that Mr. Manny died instantly. I was told his wife took the time to communicate with my attorney and my wife. The only information I could get about Mr. Manny was he worked very hard to support his family. He was a nice man all the time. One evening, on December 9, 1987, James had a few drinks at a bar, but a few turned into more. I found out he was way above the limit for drinking and driving. A few of my ex-co-workers and friends told me a picture of my car accident was on the evening news. When I spoke to my wife, she let me know the news has been broadcasting my accident. Next, she heard the telephone ring about midnight, and she was told to go visit her husband at trauma unit at Cooper Hospital. "Your husband has been involved in a serious car accident," she was told. Suddenly, she remembered seeing an accident on the newscast earlier.

I begin receiving gifts every day from all sorts of people. All of this sympathy was beginning to make me feel sad. The biggest problem was that I couldn't understand why nobody trusted me. I did not see any bruises or deep scars on my forehead. When any person seemed to stir me the wrong way, I would find myself getting into a very long, drawn-out argument over having a brain injury.

"Sam, you have so many major problems with your thinking," they said. "For some reason you cannot slow yourself down. We all can notice your brain is moving much faster than before."

As time moved on, I found out several of my relatives didn't want me to come over their houses until they knew I was getting help from a rehab hospital. During this time, my wife and I had more than enough bad vibes going on between us, and I only felt happy with her when we made love together. Other areas of our marriage were changing rapidly. Simply just being around Kathy, I would get angry. Every single reaction we had towards each other were hateful ones; she told me I made her scared. The kind of things Kathy would be doing made me agitated. So many times, I had to sit down to gather my thoughts again. Kathy and I both had a little trouble at this point with our brains, and we both needed to see a marriage counselor together. But I knew there was no way I could get Kathy to visit with a counselor. She became upset, telling me I should only make an appointment for myself. My next approach was to raise my voice, and I shoved her towards our water-bed and expressed to her, "Honey, we need to go and discuss our frustrations with professional authorities. You and I never get any chances to share time together alone."

Something was wrong with me, and every moment that went by I felt upset within myself. I just wanted to express my anger towards anything. Wow, I just could never imagine my thoughts inside my head were moving around so swiftly. Most of the time, I felt as if I had headaches coming back and forth. I took care of this pain by taking Bufferin aspirin. My mind and body enjoyed the reaction of relief from tension and pain that Bufferin gave. It also soothed headaches for millions who had tried it. Apparently this aspirin became addictive; it was the only way I could keep comfortable from the chaos around me.

Being this way really distraught the hell out of me. When I would shout at anybody, it was easy to feel such a vibration through my head. To get any release from all my agony, I called the best professional that wouldn't mind talking with me on anything. Dr. Creedon, a very good chiropractor from Cherry Hill, New Jersey, and an excellent person to tell people about the physical parts of the body. He didn't know anything about the brain but could help me find out places in my body that would cause any difficulties. Whenever I visited with Dr. Creedon at his office, whatever was bothering me would go away after he treated just a few pressure points to ease the struggle going inside my body. If there was any anger, it all went away. It simply felt like I had a normal mind once I left Dr. Creedon's office. He always mentioned brand new ideas, making me feel so much joy and happiness within myself.

A month later, I got information on where they were planning to send me for rehabilitation treatment, which was was some place in Texas.

My favorite cousin Pam shared her thoughts on this problem with me. Every afternoon, she would bring her two sons with her to visit with me at my mother's home. Our discussion would be over how proud we were for being so close. Pam talked with me the most out of anyone. It somehow felt that when Pam and I began our conversations, my mind would become much more clear, just by sharing all of the good old days of our life stories, even from our childhood days. One of the main things she had to say was not to get myself upset over what's going on.

"It's not worth the trouble. You were in a coma, which you knew nothing about. Please don't be mad at me for telling you this, but I tried talking with you the day after you were out of your, coma." My cousin let me know how I did recognize her right off. She did express to me, "Most of the time you talked too much and your conversation didn't relate to anything."

She told me my mind was just moving too quickly, so she was glad to see her cousin doing things again and up with a smile upon his face.

"Believe me," she whispered, "I cried all night thinking and praying for you. Your wife wouldn't let anyone in our family get close to you. It didn't impress anybody how she acted. I personally wanted to let her know what sort of relationship we had as cousins, but her reactions were negative for having any kind of conversations. Your wonderful mother, my lovely aunt, and I were trying our best to find out the real cause of your accident, but each time your wife would stop us from getting any source of documentation to help us all understand what part of your brain needed the most attention. The majority of us in the family hated her for doing this. It's sort of good you didn't know anything regarding what was being done. No doubt you would have been cursing everyone out big time.

"One main problem I noticed was that you had no more patience with anything, like you did before this accident happened. This was so hard to imagine. I know that you were always one of the most patient people I've ever met. All together you looked fine, like nothing ever happened. Once in a while your tone of voice would get much louder than before. Trust me, you scared a lot of people. Hardly anybody could talk with you besides your best cousin Pam. Your response was good to everything. It was terrific to see you smile the whole time we talked.

"But soon as you heard noise from anywhere, it would irritate you so badly. Suddenly, it would get hard to discuss a subject. Noticing this, I said, "let's go for a ride,.'"

So Pam and her favorite cousin went for a ride. Our first stop would be at one of our main fast food places, Kentucky Fried Chicken. She and I sat and talked for a long while and ate delicious fried chicken. Once we finished our meal, we just sat back and thought about on how to handle all the aggravation. Next, we drove around, passing by the Cooper River in Pennsauken, New Jersey, where you can see a wonderful view of the skyline of the city of Philadelphia and also the two bridges that go in and out of the city, Walt Whitman and the Ben Franklin. I was thinking it felt better just being outdoors, looking at people walking along the river and others sitting down by the river watching the canoes go up and down and the great different fowl flying above the water. It was such a sight to see air planes also flying above and across Cooper River.

As Pam drove us back, I couldn't keep myself still as she was driving, moving around too much and talking too fast. I was totally frustrated on the way back home.

My cousin told me, "Go inside and lay down. Read, relax to the sounds of jazz music. That should help your mind feel better. Try it let me know how you feel later. Call me tomorrow or this week. I'll always love you, don't forget, Chuck." (Chuck is my nickname; I've been called that throughout my life.) "You have been through a lot. God blessed you to come out of that coma… It's so hard to believe you're alive and moving around.

"We all thought, you weren't going to make it. This was one of the first times I've ever noticed all the family come together in one spirit. As you can tell, you are important to all of us. It was very difficult for anyone to get along during all the confusion over what should happen for you to get back to normal, and what I really see is that you're caught up between all the nonsense going on. Most of all, your friends and family believe you are okay until someone tries to get the best of you, then you explode with anger, and it would be hard for you to control your thinking."

My cousin Pam helped me even more to remember some things. She brought up things from the past; the majority of our conversations dealt with our childhood, as we grew up together. My memory would certainly last for a time, until an up to date question came up, and then suddenly, I couldn't remember anything. Somehow my brain just shut itself down. I often had to choose whether to see things in person to remember or rely on hearing any good information from the most concerned people that I could trust during this crucial time period in my life.

A few days later, I went to visit my wife. She ignored everything. I tried to let her know I felt disgusted being married; I just couldn't get anywhere with communication in the relationship. I sat in our bedroom watching my afternoon gameshows and writing a few business letters informing lots of my previous customers around the country what I was going through and what happened. My wife came upstairs behind me, and she mentioned to me not to use the phone to call anywhere or she would have me put out of the house.

I said to her, "What is your freaking problem, Kathy? We have never been this way towards each other."

If there was a problem, we would always straighten it out by sitting down and holding one another, talking and kissing the entire time when we had any kind of differences. We always made anything work when we put our best foot forward.

"Believe me, sweetheart, I need time away from everybody, so I can concentrate on what I need to do in order to work through this injury," I said. "You're not helping your husband at all, Honey, to understand what the real difficulties may be. Your pushing me away from you and the family.

"Believe me, Babe, no one knows what I'm going through inside my brain. Night and day, I've been trying to get along with you and explain how I feel about this accident." As much as I could realize, I continued getting sort of a neutral response from my wife. She didn't want to believe in her husband anymore.

A couple of days later, I made a call to Hanover Insurance, trying to get further information on where they were planning to send me for rehabilitation treatment. The answer I continued to receive was some place in Texas, where I would get all the help that was needed for my specific type of traumatic brain injury.

My next question for the claims adjuster was, "Why can't your company or a doctor tell me exactly what's wrong with my brain?" I was agitated by not knowing the true story that was going on. During the past four months, I had been through a lot of hell, back and forth, and never could get any source of information from anywhere. Being inquisitive, I wanted to learn more about my brain injury, and why people started saying lots of bull shit, stating, "Sam has serious problems." Whenever I found out who started these rumors, they would pay for the damages, which caused a great amount of mental cruelty.

A month later, I found out some great details from Dr. Stanley Seaton when I arrived in San Marcos, Texas. After looking over my medicine chart, he discovered all of the meds that I came to his program on. They were not the type of pills I should be taking for the type of traumatic brain injury I sustained. During my meeting with Dr. Seaton, my rehab nurse Sue Emerick attended, also hearing all the information concerning my medication. I needed a much better type of medicine to help me regain my memory, judgement, and cognitive thinking and to help my frontal lobe that was damaged. The doctor said he would start me off on 450 milligrams of lithium to slow my thinking process down a bit.

All of a sudden, I realized there was no going back home to New Jersey. I was now in the state of Texas, confused as ever. When I was able to make a phone call home, I reached my father's closest brother, Governor Sherman, and he explained to me, "It was the right idea that you went to Texas for further help after you experienced brain trauma. Tangram will help you get over the agitation inside your brain, along with working with you to problem solve again."

The program at Tangram has the kind of setting to work with people with any and all kinds of behavior. Tangram Rehab Network has developed wonderful structured facilities for traumatic brain injured people.

Finally, it was May 9, 1988, and I was an official client of the Tangram Network. I was admitted to the camp program for clients with very strong behavior and anger difficulties. My self-esteem was so low during that period of time. Trying to remember what I did every day was so terrible, and my thoughts inside my brain were not working anymore. It was hard to figure out why I had this trouble. What was wrong with me, and why did it feel like darts were being thrown at me? Why couldn't I be left alone? This feeling that I had was very discouraging.

One of the main things I prayed was for no one or nothing to bother me and make me become agitated. Living around a group of guys with head injuries became very annoying. In that place, everything was done by arrangements. As I begin to learn, the type of program I was in involved your day being structured and writing in your own notebook to remember what you're doing throughout the day. The program director required that all clients follow their structured schedule and be on time, or else you wouldn't get paid for that particular part of the program. I truly had to adjust to see God, who wants you and everyone else to be happy about your problems so you can learn to trust in his divine love! She let me know not to concentrate on what people wanted to say about my head injury, to forget all the negative talk and focus on the future, on how could I get better now that I have a weakness all throughout my body.

Brain trauma was a new experience for doctors, lawyers, and hospitals all around the country, except for Dr. Stanley Seaton who was originally from the Big D.T., which is known as Dallas, Texas. Dr. Seaton truly had the right concept to work with brain-injured people.

As I begin to learn how this structured system was operated, I begin to understand what I had to do every day in order to handle my own personal life while I lived in a brain injury facility. At times, it was very difficult trying to talk with staff about certain matters on understanding why I had to be there and be treated with such aggressiveness. Day by day, my mind started feeling a little more comfortable with being around brain-injured human beings. I begin to move on through the program, meeting new clients and staff members. Somehow taking this medicine called lithium was getting my thoughts in order again. I drank loads of water at intervals of times. My mind and body did a terrific job on handling this medicine, and that, along with Tangram's structured program, helped me to remain focused throughout the day!

Never would I imagine how many people had a brain injury from all across the United States and also from other specific countries, such as Canada. It began to be very interesting meeting other clients just like myself with a frontal lobe brain injury. Each and every day, my brain seemed to realize what I was going through. The whole entire day at Tangram was designed to get brain-injured people to function at all levels. Having to be around over 300 hundred brain injured human beings was so confusing most of the time. At intervals of time, it became a little interesting, participating in the Tangram network and having to write things down in a small notebook, which clients had to have with them at all times, so they would be able to look back on their notes with the hours that they did their responsibilities during your structured day! Many of the clients were very angry at themselves and the staff, trying to figure out what was going on throughout the working day. That's the reason we had had to write in our notebooks in order to remember all of the things we did during the work day period.

I began to have such an outstanding relationship with one the program managers. His name was Mario Gutierez, and he began to confide in me, letting me know how much he liked my attitude as a client. Mario was well liked at his program, called the Maxwell House, in which I was a client of his after I left the ranch program that his brother Ronny Gutierez was in charge of.

Later on in my structured program, Mario introduced me to the game of golf. He took me to Austin, Texas, to purchase a set of used golf clubs. Once I began to practice with these Wilson clubs, it started to become somewhat interesting, swinging at a little white golfball. When I would have any free time from my structured program, I would go outside and practice my golf swing on the program grounds, where the grass always stayed looking its best, for most of us brain-injured clients had to keep the program grounds as clean and neat as possible. The individuals that could use a lawn mower and the weed-eater machines had to get out and mow the lawn, as directed by staff, in order to get paid for that part of the workday, also to have enough token dollars to pay for your own meals and for your bed at night once you recall your day by memory at the end of your structured workday. Perhaps if you didn't make enough token money throughout your work day at the end of the pay period, when the staff is having you recall your day with male or female staff, all of us clients would have to pick a specific project to do so that we would have enough tokens money to pay for rent and board for that particular night.

Each new day at the Tangram program was about the same; the only difference was on a Monday, which was our planning and arrangement meeting, where all of us clients were given a planning and arrangement sheet to set up any plans in our program for the new week. It could be an outing with staff, or if a client were in the proper color category, which was the color yellow, they would be able to go out to eat with the group after bowling on Wednesday. This was a privilege given from the doctor and director. Depending upon a client's capabilities, once you entered Tangram you strated at the bottom in which was the color red. There weren't many privileges in the red category; about the only minor thing certain clients could do was to make one telephone call per week to whomever they chose to call: family members, or friends.

Trying to go through the program daily was such a difficult task. As I paid close attention to my program, I found out what staff personnel I could get along with so I wouldn't be afraid to communicate with them, so I could get better understanding of what brain injury is about. Now that I was living in the state of Texas, I thought I really should find out what brain trauma consisted of even more. Even though I had been through a brain trauma myself, I still wanted more insight of what this brain injury facility was trying to teach, in order for me to gain some knowledge on how anyone's brain should function being involved with a structured program on a daily basis. Dr. Stanley Seaton would have a two-week review with all his treatment units in order to find out how many of us clients reached any of our two-week goals, and also how much progress each one of us clients had made in order for him to move us on further to a new treatment facility for further stability.

Several of us clients were all the time acting stubborn and didn't want to listen to the information that was given by staff. What would be the case, perhaps if a client refused to take down notes or be on time? The consequence was being sent outside, away from the program until you got yourself and your memory in order, but to get back into the structured program, you would have to earn your way back in to the program and try to catch up with the rest of the clients in order to continue earning the token money that was provided by the Tangram Network.

Somehow, I was so confused about being involved with a brain injury program all the way in the state of Texas. I began to make a few friends with clients and staff members, but it was so different having to follow a schedule hour by hour with brain-injured people. I had always been used to not following any type of schedule, being a sales person prior to having this type of accident. My life was going through such a big change like never before.

There were only five staff that I began to have a certain level of communication with. The main person from the time I arrived was Carlton Robinsion. He always would have me ride into town with him to Seguin, Texas, to get supplies for the unit I was in at the time. Never did he put me down just because I had a brain injury. Then, I came into another staff person. Her name was Laurie Mattews; she was my P.I.C., Personal Information Coordinator. She helped with all of my cognitive matters. Laurie begin to show me how to properly balance a checkbook. Part of my structure was to have a checkbook meeting with her on Mondays after I finished with the arrangement meeting from writing down all plans for the new week.

For a good little while at Tangram, I started to become relaxed. All of a sudden, I came across a terrific staff member by the name of Darrell Madkins. He sat me down and said he could help me out with writing in my journal at five o'clock each day during the structure until I regained my memory back.

As long as I took my meds on time and followed my schedule, he would teach me how to get out into the community, plus we could start going to concerts in Austin, Texas.

Darrell stated, "Don't let me down, Sam. Everybody is here for your benefit to get you well, so you can be on your way back home to New Jersey. Hang in there, Sam, you'll see several changes in yourself in about six months, so don't give up, no matter what. The staff will be right there to keep you going and help you be active within the program.

"Sam what's hard for you to understand is that your brain needs to settle down and heal itself. After your injury, most of the cell walls in your brain have been damaged. Initially, you would become angry and destructive with property when you would encounter problems. Sam, most of the staff notices that frequently, you interrupt when we're providing information or directions towards other clients."

Laurie said, "Sam, you have a bad problem doing this. Most of all we're seeing difficulty accepting the rules and limits. For some apparent reason, you cannot accept responsibility for your actions. All you do, Sam, is blame others for your mistakes. Dr. Stanley Seaton has suggested for you to demonstrate and improve your ability to control your impulses and decrease being negative and making sarcastic comments before Tangram transfers you to our prevocational program.

"Based on your current level of progress, we estimate that you will be able to transfer into another program within eight to ten months. Without any doubt, you have achieved gradual gains in a structured rehabilitation setting, and you have a very good prognosis for further improvement."

I believed my wife and rehab nurse should participate in the Tangram staff conference to determine if my goals were being met and how long I should continue treatment at the Tangram Network.

"Sam has strong potential for a good recovery perhaps, if he can be treated in a strong behaviorally-oriented, highly-structured program. The admission evaluation shows you have a strong vocational background and intellect, which makes you an excellent candidate for further rehabilitation."

I received a telephone call from my wife, and the first words from her mouth were, "Sam, I'm so glad you made up your mind to go get help down in Texas. We all miss you and want you to get better from all this confusion. Dr. Seaton let me know not to visit with you right away. About four to six months, that's what he prefers. Everyone has noticed your agitation level is at a very high level now. The best thing for you now is to keep away from any trouble."

Over and over again, I stated, "Perhaps if I meant anything to you as a husband, you wouldn't tell me so many negative things. Believe me, sweetheart, I want this marriage to last always and forever. I want to see you before six months go by; there's no damn way I'll let anything keep us from being together. Let us hang up now, my love, I'm tired of talking about this nonsense shit over the telephone. Call me as soon as you can; I want out of this rehab place. Stop all the sympathy bullshit, and buy a first class ticket from United Airlines or Delta, so I can leave.

Why should I stay in a place that I dislike, my dear? You're so slow with the times; people don't put up with such bullshit from mankind now-a-days. It's all about hurt or kill someone, so let's both get off this trip and come back to reality, Kathy. We need each other desperately, so don't let rehabilitation keep us apart."

Meanwhile in the background, all I could hear was, "Get off the phone, Sam, your time is up. There is a ten-minute time limit for everyone, so don't get irritated about that. It's a rule for all of the clients to follow."

A staff member by the name of Shad Williams, walked in and shouted, "Sam, when the staff tells you to hang-up the phone, do it, or we will take you outside, so just get the hell off when we ask you to please."

Shad told me, "Listen my brother, I'll be here in the program often to help you with any problem you might have. So don't feel afraid to ask for help when I'm around. Carlton and Big Bill can also give you lots of assistance. Believe me, Sam, we all are here to help you overcome this traumatic experience. Right now, my man, you can't go anywhere, Look at all the surroundings, how will you try to escape? There's no way out. Tangram has you covered.

"Why won't you let anyone help you through this problem? The state of New Jersey wanted to send you in our direction at Tangram, the best place in the world to treat head injuries that any of us knows of. We want you to stop worrying about leaving Tangram; we're here to help, you much as possible.

"We have heard them all before, so I'm just letting you know no one here is bothered by your actions. Stay cool and the best thing you could do for me is watch the language you use around everything. If I hear any other curse words from you, my decision will be to keep you outside working away from the rest of the clients. None of these people need to hear profanity; this would create too much tension for this type of group."

At this point and time, I felt disgusted just hearing about injuries or simply seeing any damage, or noticing any kind of human injuries. My brain was confused. How did I get into this mess? No one could tell me a true answer of why I needed rehabilitation. Later during the week, I was asked to go with a staff member into Seguin, Texas, to pick up hardware. The program needed new locks for the barn doors, tool room, and safety cabinets. Carlton Robinson let me know I would be riding with him to pick up supplies.

"No funny bullshit, Sam, or I will take you to our hollow. Believe this or not, you won't like it down there, living at the hollow. Keeps you from being agitated around the clients and staff. If anyone gets sent there, they will work their way back into the program. Staff will see that a client is ready to return with the group by knowing that person has calmed down.

I want to tell you this, I've thought of a nickname that fits you to a tee. From now on, Mr. C will call you Sam Sausage. Now promise me, no problems while we're in town. If there should be, once we get back I will check in with the manager Rick Mallard, and you won't be trusted to go into town for a long time. One month at least."

My comment to Mr. C, "Do you think I really care about this ignorant idea concerning rehabilitation. It's such a weird feeling I have not to realize I've been through brain trauma. What can I do Mr. C? There's nothing I've seen that can get me to accept that I have a brain injury. I sure hope and pray this place will help me understand any problems I have. As I've told everyone, this will be the last rehabilitation treatment I will go to.

"Perhaps if someone tries and put me anywhere else, they will surely regret it, for I'll curse them out so bad they'll feel like shit. However, I won't be in the mood to hear anymore jive talk on rehab."

One of my favorite staff members Laurie Mattews helped me realize why I should stay at Tangram for a while. She gave more than enough of her time working side by side with each client. To me, her attitude was very sweet. Too bad, so sad that I was in a rehab unit; I would have asked her out for a date.

"Sam, how would your wife feel if you asked a girl out for a date? She'd probably come all the way to Texas and slap your face! Stop causing these type of problems." Tangram doesn't believe in relationships with the opposite sex until a client earns his or her privilege in what Tangram calls the appropriate color category. The basic idea of the program is to get clients to learn how they should earn something before it's given to them. Why does a person need to go through this sort of punishment? The majority of all head injuries are caused by the other guy. A few studies have shown very little therapy is known for anyone who has a brain injury. The majority of the treatment centers located on the East coast aren't up-to-date with brain injuries. It is estimated that in the United States each year, one million cases of head injuries require hospitalization. For the longest time clinicians dealing with brain-injured patients had been under the assumption that once a brain-injury victim passes through the spontaneous recovery phase, there is little that can be done to assist a patient with recovery because brain damage is permanent.

This isn't a joking matter. Anyone that has a head injury needs to find out as much as he or she can from medical professionals. Most of the latest information proves doctors are becoming more familiar with head-injured patients.

No one believes me, but I can do just about anything that anyone else can do. The majority of the time, I do better than most people. What's so mind boggling is that not a single person has one bit of information on the exact thing wrong with my head. I'm having a hard time believing that anything is wrong inside my head. Doctors at the University of Pennsylvania's x-rays and evaluations show no signs of brain injury, just one report showing tissue scarring over the left eye, mainly where the impact occurred from the accident. More evaluations would be needed to be sure everything is okay with all the brain tissue. A true head injured patient right away would strike out at someone. It was getting so difficult to live with all sorts of people this way. My only intention was to avoid problems with anyone under the head-injury syndrome. What was the matter with this picture? I couldn't focus my thoughts at all on being a head trauma individual. The main thing I would hear several doctors mention was the nervous system controls the actions and sensations of all the parts of your body, as well as your thoughts, emotions, and memories. How would this problem be solved? I had no idea or clue where to go or who to talk with. Finding out information on brain injury is tough for just about anyone.

Calling legal people was a joyful experience. Why wouldn't anyone in the legal field know some of the answers to my questions? I felt a whole load of disappointment in my heart from this painful experience. About the only way I could make myself feel comfortable was to shout out words when something or someone caused me to get extremely agitated, I tend to shout out words of aggression. . It felt as though I had no relief from any of the disruption going on with my life. Brain injury is very hard to relate to. I was experiencing nothing but pure loneliness within myself. It was so uncomfortable living this way. It was just like a person living all alone in this big, round world. No one could ever know what I really was experiencing inside.

All of a sudden, my wife let me know I was getting ready to leave San Marcos, Texas, soon. She had found a place closer to home. The name of this rehab is called Beechwood in Langhorne, Pennsylvania. Several weeks later, a director from Beechwood came down to Tangram network to interview me. His name was Dr. Fellicetti, and he told me he liked how I looked, and I would be a good client for Beechwood services. So afterwards, I met with my Personal Information Coordinator to go over all excessive medical bills from my auto accident that my wife didn't pay while I was in Texas. I found out I had $3,000 worth of medical bills that were not paid, and I had to pay those bills myself before I left the state of Texas.

Dr. Seaton informed me, "Sam, your wife needed $1,000 to help her pay some of the bills at home in New Jersey."

I mentioned to the doctor, "My wife is already getting all of my money to pay the bills, so why do I need to send her my money from Tangram, for my income here is very minimal.

All that I was told by the doctor and staff was, "Sam, send the money home to your wife. Write a check and Laurie will sign it with you."

Then I realized I had no other choice but to send this $1,000 check home to Kathy. She didn't need any more money in her possession in New Jersey; she refused to pay my medical bills and left me stuck with all sorts of bills from San Antonio, Austin, San Marcos, and Gonzalez. I paid all of those past due medical bills through Balcones Bank in San-Marcos, Texas. Somehow, I completed all of those past-due bills without any disruptions or complaints. I called my attorney in Woodbury, New Jersey, to inform him the main reason that I had to do what was necessary for my treatment in order to leave the Tangram Network.

At this point of my rehab life in Texas, I was really liking Texas very much. Every day, it was extremely hot, and I mean hot, weather. I drank lots of water very consistently because I was off the medicine called lithium, in which was a very good pill for the type of brain injury I sustained. That was one of the best ideas Dr. Stanley Seaton did for yours truly, to prescribe that particular medication. I was a very balanced person after I would take this medication. No one or nothing could interrupt me whatsoever. I kept my conversation on a good level with all sorts of people, staff and clients, also even professionals. I was able to focus on one thing at a time really well.

The majority of the people that knew me sort of noticed I was improving from my brain injury since I began taking lithium. All I kept hearing from every one of my fellow co-workers was, "Samuel, why are you drinking so much water all the time?"

My reply was, "I'm taking some sort of salt-pill which it makes my mouth get real dry fast, and I become dehydrated all the time."

The manager's wife of the Mesa-Verda, Patricia Gutierez, brought me a very large water jug to carry with me all day to keep me from trying to find a water fountain to drink water because of the medication's affect. Lithium was slowing my thinking process down very much, and all I knew was that it was really working for my traumatic brain injury. My cognitive parts of my brain became well on its own all of a sudden. Somehow, my attention span, focus, and abilities were all in place, thank God.

During this period of my life, I seem to be straight as an arrow. My mind, body, and soul was balanced; nothing at all could distract my attention. Several of my good memories were returning to me, especially the great thoughts my grandfather Joesph Morgan and the things he would say to me. It was so great to remember each day that I would come home from high school, and my wonderful grandfather would be waiting for me in the backyard at my parents home in Lawnside, New Jersey, to talk with me about many different things in life.

Tangram network refused to let me go on a home pass to see my mother, my lovely grandfather, and my son, even though my brain was in much better condition than from the beginning of my head injury. Things were looking better and better day-by-day for me to get my guardianship back from my wife, Kathleen. The doctor still didn't feel as though I was ready to handle my own affairs after all of the rehabilitation treatment I have been through since the very beginning, which started back in 1988. What a mess! It had been for ten years already of being away from my wife and step-children, along with my family members. This would be a true statement. Many men who sustained a brain injury as myself would have done something very harmful by now, or hurt someone, or hurt themselves. They could have been attempting to jump off a bridge, maybe even take an over-dose of any drugs or, alcohol, or just simply run away. Tangram was located in a nice rural area of central Texas. I truly believe I kept my composure the whole entire ten years of being in that structured program that was designed as a puzzle with missing pieces, trying to put the brain all back together from a bad head injury, either from a bad automobile accident or work-related injuries, etc.

Tangram Rehabilitation Network Services again located in San Marcos, Texas, between Austin and San Antonio, Main Highway is I35, will never be forgotten. I had to manage my life for ten long years without my wife; I don't believe that the average person could have put up with all of the non-sense bullshit this structured network had to offer. Several individuals made it their own decision to just get up and leave Tangram. Clients would decide to run away when the program would take us out on Sunday outings, or when any of the programs would attend a rodeo in Austin, and even when we went out for dinner on Wednesday evenings after bowling, someone just would take off from the group and their specific partners.

Jennifer Neeb, my claim's adjuster for Hanover out of Piscataway, New, Jersey, After all of those years in Texas, several good things that kept my attention span at a great level: going on outings to play golf, seeing those Texas rodeos, eating steak, beef, and chicken fajiatas, and most of all visiting Austin, which is the capital of Texas. It's such a great looking city with lots of fun and excitement, beautiful scenery, and lots of outdoor activities. In Austin, it's fun, fun, fun in the Lone Star State! It's such a large state, with miles and miles of highway, land, hillside country, cattle, cows, sheep, and goats, etc. As one of their old sayings goes, after living in Texas for a period of time, it will quickly grow on you. Also, as anyone should know, it gets very dry and hot in the Lone Star State. It hardly ever rains in Texas, but boy, oh boy, when it does rain, it really pours down so hard and long and fast, all the traffic on the road has to stop. Everything on the highway has to pull over, as there is no visibility. You have to wait until the rain really, truly stops!

During this last period of time in Texas, I was getting very excited that I would be going home, back to New Jersey, to be with my wife and family, plus my mother and son. It felt so good inside of my body and mind to know I was going back to the east coast where I was born and raised. I just couldn't wait to see the Sherman family, along with all of my former coworkers, high school friends, and all of the church people in my township. I went around to say goodbye to all of the clients at the townhouse program, the Mesa Verda where my golfing buddy and manager at the mesa was in charge. I spoke to my former coworkers that were clients at the Tangram nursery. I most certainly had to go to Quail Creek Country Club in beautiful San Marcos, not that far from Texas and where the Aggies are from!

It has been such a great experience being in the Lone Star State of Texas. I met lots of good people while in the Tangram Rehab Network. Several people in the program, I will always try to keep in-touch with them, and half of the community of San Marcos I considered family and friends.

I will also always remember my ten-year journey while at Tangram Network. Dr. Stanley Seaton knew a hell-of-a-lot of information about traumatic brain injuries. The only time I had any difficulties with Dr. Seaton was when he refused to let me leave his program to go back and visit my wife, mother, and any of the Sherman family. My wife Kathy and Dr. Seaton were hand-in-hand on refusing to let me be on my own after spending many years at Tangram. Not one time did I visit my wife Kathy in Jersey; all she would say to me is that she was taking care of the house and my personal affairs, stop thinking about what she was doing, and just worry about my rehab. Never one time did my wife say, "Honey I want you home with me, so we can do some of the things we use to do together."

I left from the Austin Airport and headed back to my hometown on the East Coast. I flew back on my favorite airline, which is Delta Airlines. I arrived in Philadelphia International Airport, and two staff members from Beechwood Sevices met me. It was two women, Arlene and Sarah. I saw two name badges and a sign with the name of the new rehab. My wife Kathy didn't even come to greet her own husband upon arrival back home. That goes to show what type of so-called wife I had married. She just only wanted to have control over me and all of my affairs in life so that she could handle all of the money that I was receiving from my structured settlement.

Soon after being at Beechwood Program, I was really beginning to enjoy being back home in the Pennsylvania/New Jersey area. It was such a very different look and surrounding being in the Langhorne, Pennsylvania, a neat location to reside. Now I realized I was at a well put together rehab for brain injuries. The staff members and the doctors all gave you the time to go over your thoughts and feelings about your personal brain injury.

Once the psychologist at Beechwood, Dr. Thomas Blash, stated, "Sam, how did they declare you to be an incompetant person?"

Dr. Blash repeated, "Sam, I really mean this when I say this statement, you're the most competent person that I've ever done a competency evaluation on. Why did that doctor keep you in Texas so long without giving you your guardianship back?"

The way I responded to that question towards Dr. Blash was by saying that Dr. Seaton just continued to tell me that my wife Kathy would tell him I disturb her too much during the night. All I was trying to do was communicate with her so I could come to a point to bring me back home, out of Texas. Any human being would get lonley after long periods of time going by being without their own spouse.

Weeks later, things seemed to be okay. I then found out I was a grandfather. It was such a warm welcoming home! Gifts were all over the place. One of my favorite cousins, Pam, was so happy to see me after all those years. My mother was very uplifted; she couldn't stop smiling knowing how much better I looked from the start of my traumatic brain injury. The majority of my friends had moved to different areas of New Jersey, some even left the state altogether.

After ten years of rehabilitation and living in a structured life, it made such an impact inside my brain. I was very eager to go back to work and drive a car again in Pennsylvania and New Jersey. My brain felt just fine; I was still taking my medicine, but only played golf a few times, not much as I did when I lived in San Marcos, Texas. Golf was a very big part of my success being in Tangram Rehab Network. The game helped me to focus my mind, concentrate on each shot, and helped my right-ankle, which had gotten damaged during my accident. When any golf shot goes into a sand trap, a player would have to rotate both of their feet down into the sand to get the golf ball up and out of the sand. Doing this often when I would play the game of golf, it strengthened my ankle a whole lot. Moving my legs back and forth in a sand trap really did wonders for me and my badly injured right ankle.

At various times in my life, it seemed as though no one even cared about me being independent again, only but God. I just kept talking and praying to our Father in Heaven to bless my situation and condition to get back to a normal life once again. Most of all, I just wanted to work and enjoy people. Sure, it never even felt like I had a head injury. I still felt the same way inside of my entire system. It was difficult trying to get my wife, insurance people, doctors, and lawyers to understand me at this point of my injury; no one wanted to listen, but I knew the Good Lord above was still on his throne looking down and watching over the whole entire matter. All I could do was just hold my head high and keep faith in Him, the highest of all things in this entire world.

Although I really wanted to trust Dr. Stanley Seaton at Tangram Network, who truly seemed to be a marvelous medical professional for traumatic brain injured human beings (Doc for short, as most of the staff and clients would call him at times), he only let me have one home visit back in July of 1993. The most I could say to anyone is to stay on the positive side of life when you're going through any kind of difficulty with spouses, professionals, family members, friends, co-workers, etc., because in due time things will change again in your favor. God is always standing by your side to bring things, all conditions, to a new beginning. Just remember, He will do it in His time, not yours. For He reminds us that we can do all things through Christ who strengthens us. Until this day, it is truly a spiritual blessing to still have life and an abundant one, as God's word tells us in the Bible. You can find that particular scripture in John 10:10.

Once after getting through all the mess, I finally gained a lot of independence at Beechwood Services. Thank God I was able to be back on track to work and love everything all over again by staying focused and also being around good, positive people again. What I've really learned about this whole mix-up of having a brain injury is to try your hardest not to let someone, or just any type of problem, get to you and cause any frustration from keeping your mind focused on one thing at a time. Whether it is talking, eating, driving, or working, any given subject the brain can handle, anytime day or night.

I never wanted to divorce my wife Kathy, but I did after finding out what kind of life she was living with her children, which were my stepchildren. Even now, she had a problem visiting with me at Beechwood. Most of the staff and personnel knew my wife just simply was taking advantage of me, with no respect for my family or friends to visit with me now that I was at home. What a major trip she was, just being a rip-off, gold-digger at her best towards her husband's settlement. I gave it my best with this woman I married, for better or worse and until death do us part, but I decided finally that I wanted a divorce from Kathy Sherman.

Now that Dr. Tom Blash helped me get my guardianship back from my wife Kathy, I was so ready to move forward with my life by the help of the Lord Jesus Christ and also most of the Beechwood Services professionals.

Regardless, my wife had no true love for me. When I did come to our home to stay while visiting our residence in Willingboro, New Jersey, she made me sleep in our garage, not with her for she, claiming that she wasn't feeling well and didn't want to be bothered by her husband of ten long years. I just couldn't quite figure out the real reason why Kathy stopped wanting me to be next to her after we spent a decade away from each other. All I can say about this matter is (and I never liked using these types of words), what a dirty bitch she turned out to be. After all those years apart during the 90's she still asked me for money to help her pay bills. Isn't that bitch already taking in all the cash at hand? What more did that so-called wife I married want out of her brain-that-couldn't-be-broken husband that drowned in the Lone Star State without all the love and support of a wife. Weeks and weeks ahead, I found out details that my so-called wife, who I thought was being truthful with my finances, instead took most of my funds and placed them in certain locations within New Jersey and Virginia.

But God doesn't like ugly things being done towards all of us human beings, for the Bible says, you shall reap what you sow! Suddenly after our divorce, I never knew she had kidney trouble after all of her dirty, sneaky ways. Well, Kathy didn't get too far after all enjoying the rest of her life with the money she had taken while taking complete advantage of her brain-that-couldn't-be-broken husband, Samuel. God took her away in 2004. It's so hard to imagine Katy wasn't still alive, on God's green earth, after the horrible mess she created for both of our lives as a married couple.

Learning at Beechwood Services has brought me to a wonderful way of gaining further independence in my life. Now that Dr. Nagle has taken over Beechwood neuro-rehab services, he has built a nice looking club house for all the clients to attend on a regular basis to improve their communications skills. He has also improved work-related conditions. As time continues to go ahead, the new club house at Beechwood Stabler Center will help all the head injured clients hopefully regain strong courage to continue their lives. All anyone can do is their best each day of their lives while in a facility.

Living in the Bucks County area is a great experience to be a part of. Knowing myself, I enjoy meeting lots of different people from different nationalities. Just about everywhere I would travel around the area, I would make a good friend. I was getting pretty good help along the way being with a few staff that I could relate to. I learned more about the game of golf from several great individuals. I just want everyone to always keep somewhere in their own minds: no matter if you experience a traumatic brain injury or not, your brain cannot be broken. Staying determined will help anyone make it through all the rough and tough times in life during periods of rehabilitation.

Now that I'm back in my hometown and familiar grounds, I have more support from lots of authorities, family, friends, also from a few fellow clients and staff personnel. My mother was so happy to have her son back at home, where she could drive and come visit with me. Going back around my area where I grew up was a major difference in people and all the new surroundings. For one particular reason, my mind had to adjust to everything. The biggest part of my return home was that I could drive my own self places without any supervision.

So the moral of my story is that my brain couldn't be broken from all of the traumatic trauma I experience to my head. The most accurate professionals helped me regain life in the real world again. My wonderful uncle, Joe Sherman, showed all his wonderful support towards me by attending majority of R.S.T. meetings for a six-month review of my progress. Most of my family and friends were truly thrilled to see how much I was still capable of handling myself as Sam Sherman again! I somehow began to miss certain friends of mine in the Lone Star State of Texas, most of all my former manager, Mario Gutierez, He was my true best golf buddy while I attended Tangram.

Every ounce of rehabilitation really helped me achieve my independence.

Foremost, I give thanks to our Lord and Savior Jesus Christ for his loving kindness for keeping me alive twenty-three years later. I most certainly have to express the medicine, structure, professionals, and golf outings made it much easier to handle having an injury to my brain. Thank God, it is better with my life in general. I just want to let all human beings know that you can survive any type of difficulty in your life by just being positive. Keep a smile, think faithfully, and trust in God above because you will win the battle, for God won't let your brain ever become broken. We all are children of the King.